RUPERT GOES NORTH

One afternoon Rupert went down to the lake. He saw someone splashing about in the water.

"Help!" called a voice. "Lend me a hand. I've fallen in!"

It was Dr Botney. Rupert ran to help him out.

"Thank you, Rupert," said the doctor, climbing on to the grass.

Dr Botney was a famous collector. He collected plants from all over the world.

"I'm going to the North Pole tomorrow," he told Rupert. "Would you like to come with me?"

"Yes, please!" said Rupert, clapping his hands. "My Uncle Polar lives there. I could visit him."

The next day, Rupert met Dr Botney at the lake. The doctor was dressed in a flying suit.

"Are we going to get there by plane?" asked Rupert.

"Yes, in my yellow sea-plane!" said Dr Botney, proudly.

Rupert was excited.

It was a long journey. Rupert looked out of the window all the way. At last he could see some land.

"We're here," said Dr Botney. He brought the plane down gently.

"I'll go and collect some plants now," said the doctor.

"And I'll visit Uncle Polar," said Rupert. "He will be surprised!"

Rupert thought he knew the way. But the land was covered in snow. Everywhere looked the same!

Then Rupert heard someone calling him. It was Sailor Sam, here to do some fishing.

"Your uncle's home is just over that hill," said Sam, pointing.

Rupert was glad when he reached his uncle's home. He was soon inside, out of the icy wind.

Uncle Polar gave Rupert a cup of warm milk. And Rupert told him all about Dr Botney and his trip in the yellow sea-plane.

When the sky got dark, Rupert knew it was time to leave. So he pulled on his gloves and his winter coat. And he set off through the snow, back to Dr Botney.

"Take care, Rupert!" called Uncle Polar, waving. "Come again soon!"

It was much harder going back. There was a strong wind. And big flakes of snow blew in Rupert's face. He was very pleased to see Sailor Sam running towards him.

"It's a snowstorm!" said Sam. "We can shelter in my boat."

Rupert and Sailor Sam ran to Sam's little boat. They got in and sheltered from the storm.

Suddenly there was a bang! The wind lifted the boat and it crashed into a huge lump of ice. Luckily, Rupert and Sam weren't hurt. But the boat was broken.

Soon the storm was over. Sailor Sam looked at his broken boat.

"How will I get home?" he said.

Then Rupert saw something in the sky. It was Dr Botney in the sea-plane! Rupert jumped up and down and waved his scarf.

"The doctor will give you a lift!" said Rupert, happily.

When they got back to Nutwood, Mr Bear was waiting. He was surprised to see Sailor Sam with Rupert and the doctor.

"Rupert's had a very cold adventure!" said Dr Botney.

"So now he needs a good, hot meal," said Mr Bear, smiling.

First published in this format in 1993 by Dean,
an imprint of Reed Consumer Books Limited,
Michelin House, 81 Fulham Road, London SW3 6RB,
and Auckland, Melbourne, Singapore and Toronto.
Rupert characters TM & © 1993 Express Newspapers plc.
Licensed by Nelvana Marketing Inc.
U.K. representatives: Abbey Home Entertainment Licensing
Text copyright © 1993 Reed International Books Limited
Artwork by Alfred Bestall from *Rupert and the Iceberg*
copyright © 1955 Express Newspapers plc
Colouring by Gina Hart copyright © 1991 Express Newspapers plc
All rights reserved.

ISBN 0 603 55178 5

Printed in Italy